K.I.N.G.D.O.M.
Series

Series 1 - Book 2

The K.I.N.G.D.O.M. Series is a series of young children's books (ages 2-8), which follows the adventures of the King's Kids. Each book in the series explores a concept or a principle, using K.I.N.G.D.O.M. as an acronym. In the second book, *King's Kids: A Day at the Beach*, the kids learn about their **I**dentity under the King.

On a warm sandy beach, waves brushing the shore,
Were four sets of footprints unlike any before.
All unique but the same, these prints did proclaim
The King's Kids they're called, yet each their own name.

There was Ryan in his castle, as tall as a tree,
Washed away with the tide, Ryan's house out to sea.

After taking her swim, Abby comforted him.
"Don't be sad, Ryan. We'll build it again."

And speaking of trees, Miguel shook one and found
A big hairy shell; it then fell to the ground
Where it split open wide to reveal milk inside
For Miguel (and Duke), a yummy surprise.

And what about Kyra? Where did she go?
She swam to a big rock and ten feet below
To a place of wonder and colors so bright;
She met new friends there, to her great delight.

And rising for air, she was met with a stare
From a snake on the rock who then did declare,
"My goodness, child! You're the first I have ssseen.
And I've ssseen a lot! But never a queen."

"A pleasure to meet you," said Kyra with cheer.
"The sssame to you, but why are you here?"
"I was sent by my father to rule in this place."
"But you're just a kid – no offence, your Grace."

And the snake, full of lies and deceit in his eyes
Filled Kyra with doubts through all his advice.
With a hiss, "Little Miss, there is much more to sssee."
Then she swam back to shore, there met by Abby.

"Why the long frown? Why are you down?"
Abby asked her sister. "Kyra, pick up your crown."

15

With all gathered near, Kyra spoke of the reef,
Of the birds in the sky and the creatures beneath,
Of the crabs and the urchins, and the snake on the rock
And the things the snake said, never mind he could TALK!

"He told me I'm small, not yet worthy to sit
On a throne of my own, but he could teach me a bit.
He praised me, then mocked me, then mocked me some more;
It was all so confusing, I swam back to the shore."

And then from above a dove perched on Duke's head;
It was Alo the Helper, to all of them said,
"Kids, listen to me, do not turn or flee;
You are Kids of the King, not fish in the sea."

"You were sent by your dad and made for his pleasure
To rule in this place, now and forever."

"Thank you, Alo!" said Kyra with glee.
I had forgotten my role and identity.
I'm not just a kid -- I'm a King's Kid, by birth,
And I won't be deceived by some snake on the earth."

Then the kids joined together in songs to their dad,
Giving thanks for the day and the lesson they had.

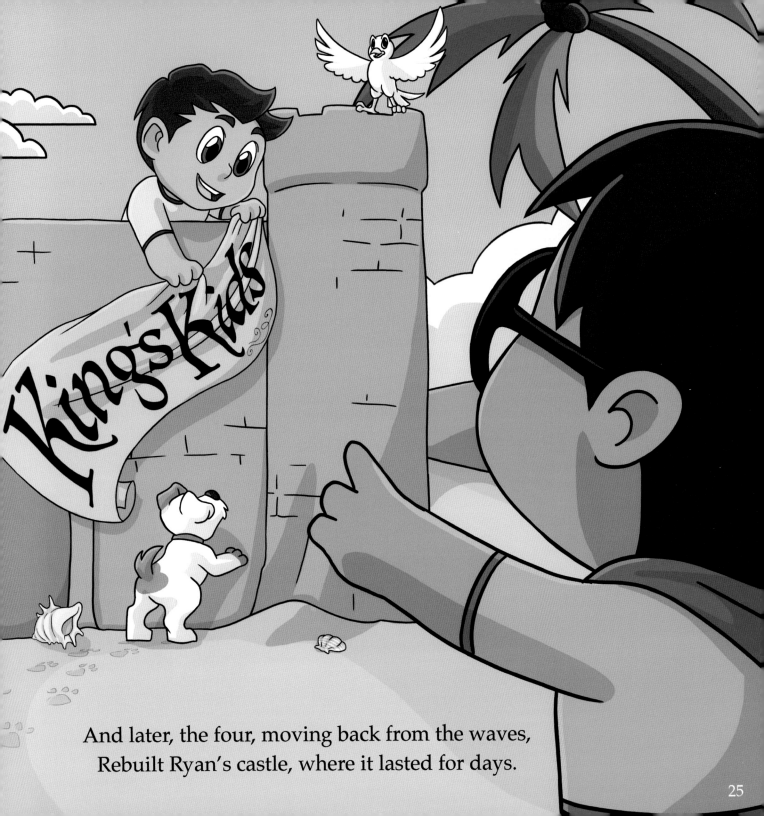

And later, the four, moving back from the waves,
Rebuilt Ryan's castle, where it lasted for days.

Keys from the King:

- • Your identity is who you are.

- • When you are born into a royal family, you are royalty.

- • You are born a King's Kid; it's who you are.

- • Your age does not determine your identity as a King's Kid.

- • No matter what anyone says or what happens to you,
  ## You are a King's Kid!

ISBN: 978-1-7334064-8-2

Written & Produced by Eric Madej, Jodi Madej, Sharrana Matulka, and Michael Matulka
Published by King's Kids Books • Illustrations by Tiffany Wilson • Color Art by Angela Kluesner
Design & Layout by Basik Studios • Written by E.L. Nance

Printed in the United States of America   *www.kingskidsbooks.com*

Honoring the Life and Legacy
of Dr. Myles Munroe